MW00966721

A Place to BLOOM

A Place to BLOOM

Lorianne Siomades

Boyds Mills Press

Text and illustrations copyright © 1997 by Lorianne Siomades
All rights reserved

Published by Bell Books
Boyds Mills Press, Inc.
A Highlights Company
815 Church Street
Honesdale, Pennsylvania 18431
Printed in China

Publisher Cataloging-in-Publication Data
Siomades, Lorianne.
    A place to bloom / by Lorianne Siomades.—1st ed.
[32]p. : col.ill. ; cm.
Summary : This picture book in rhyme asks children to look closely at the world around them.
ISBN 1-56397-656-0
1. Nature—Fiction—Juvenile literature. 2. Stories in rhyme—Juvenile literature. [1. Nature—Fiction.
2. Stories in rhyme.] I. Title.
    [E]—dc20   1997   AC   CIP
Library of Congress Catalog Card Number 96-86536
First edition, 1997

Book designed by Lorianne Siomades
The text of this book is set in 22-point Times.
The illustrations are done in cut paper and watercolor and gouache.

10 9 8 7 6 5 4

The stream I like to visit
is someone's place to drink.

It's someone else's home,
and someone's place to think.

The peas I hate upon my plate
are someone's favorite treat.

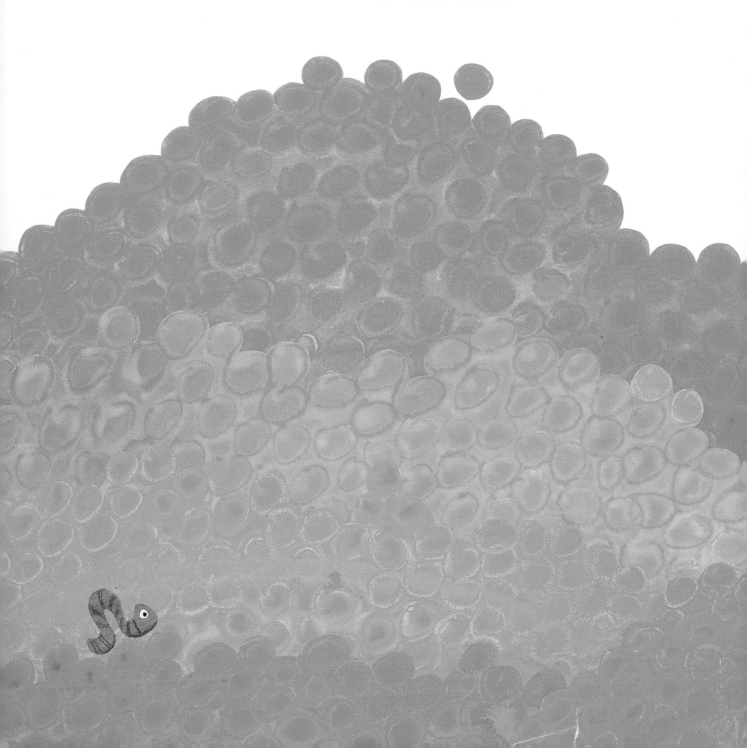

The part I usually throw away,
someone loves to eat!

The big old tree
I love to climb,
someone else enjoys.

The slippers that
I never liked
are someone's
favorite toys.

The grass I love to lay in
hides someone else's food.

Something finds a place to bloom

and someone else intrudes!

The feather that is light for me,
others cannot lift.

The breakfast on my table

is someone else's gift.

The sunny sky that lets me fly
my kite upon the breeze
is the same sky where others fly
as freely as they please.

The scary snake on the garden path
who doesn't look friendly . . .

is someone else's mother,
who is more afraid of me!

And the teddy bear that showed much wear,
that no one thought to mend,
was thrown away the very same day . . .

he became my very best friend!